Mabel

By Cotton Mathers

The moral rights of the author has been asserted

All rights reserved

No part of this publication maybe reproduced, stored in a retrieval system or transmitted in any form or by any means, without the prior permission in writing of the publisher, nor be otherwise circulated in any form of binding or cover other than that in which it is published and without a similar condition including this condition being imposed on the subsequent purchaser.

The Empire Publishers publishing
12808 West Airport Blvd Suite 270M Sugar Land, TX 77478

https://empirepublishers.co/about-us

Our books may be purchased in bulk for promotional, educational, or business use. Please contact The Empire Publishers at +(844) 636-4576, or by email at support@theempirepublishers.com

First Edition February 2024

About the Author

Cotton Mathers is the pseudonym for Shane Blanton, an accomplished author hailing from Ironton, Ohio. With a deep-rooted passion for writing horror fiction, Shane crafts tales that captivate and thrill his readers. He draws inspiration from his surroundings and life experiences, infusing his works with a unique blend of suspense and terror.

Shane's academic journey includes studies at Ohio University Southern and Ashland University, where he honed his skills and nurtured his love for storytelling. Beyond his writing, Shane is a devoted father to his daughter, Autumn Chase, who is a source of inspiration and joy in his life.

Under the name Cotton Mathers, Shane continues to pursue his passion for horror fiction, bringing spine-chilling narratives to his audience. His dedication to the craft and ability to weave intricate plots make him a standout figure in the genre.

Table of Contents

Introduction 1

Chapter One 3

Chapter Two 11

Chapter Three 23

Chapter Four 32

Chapter Five 41

Chapter Six 51

Chapter Seven 63

Chapter Eight 74

Chapter Nine 82

Chapter Ten 90

Chapter Eleven 101

Chapter Twelve 109

Introduction

Gentry Farm is stained with sorrow and tragedy from decades before. This property holds a secret that is buried deep in the past. Mabel Gentry haunts not only this property but also the psyche of the new property owners. John and Emma Tyler are unaware of the farm's history and the cries for help from the ghostly victim who once lived on this side. John and Emma struggle to maintain their sanity while looking to start a life on their new farm. Mabel Gentry will remain in John and

Emma's world unless they realize their help is needed. The profound experience the couple will endure proves to them that a mother's love reaches far beyond the grave.

Chapter One

Baby Meredith has been missing for six weeks. All search parties have called off their searches. Every vacant lot and overgrown plot of land has been thoroughly scoured tirelessly. Even the heavily forested areas have been combed over with cadaver dogs, the sheriff's department, and teams of volunteers in the hopes that a clue or piece of evidence may turn up a lead in the disappearance of the eighteen-month-old little girl.

The daily dispatch ran its last story on the disappearance on June 6, 1967. Since then, the small farming community of Proctorville, Ohio, has been rocked with grief and horror over the crime that has left everyone reeling for answers. Baby Meredith is not the only thing missing from the community; the slow-paced and rural town's sense of safety and security is also missing.

Theodore and Mabel Gentry have barely slept or eaten since the disappearance of their first and only child. Theodore spends his days holding the hand of his broken and grief-stricken wife, Mabel, and spends his nights drinking hard liquor to cope with the loss and to numb the wound it has inflicted.

Theodore and Mabel are complete opposites. Theodore is a large man with a six-foot frame, broad-shouldered, hardened, and heavily muscled from a lifetime of hard labor and the stubbornness of a mule. Mabel is a small, petite woman with long black hair, dark as coal. Her voice is as soft and meek as her demeanor. The sundress she was wearing the morning she realized her daughter was missing out of her nursery is now too large to fit her fragile and emaciated body. Mabel Gentry is grieving herself to death.

Gentry Farm consists of a two-story Victorian-era home with turned-style pillars. Decorative corbels adorn the eaves of the pitched roof and dormer windows that jut out from the turret tower with a spiral roof. A prairie barn and horse corral sit on the south end of the sprawling twelve-acre farm with a slow-running creek that drains into a babbling brook just before you get to the thicket of pine trees that mark the property line on the western side of the livestock pasture. Picturesque middle American perfection is how Gentry Farm was described until tragedy cut deep into the fabric of the Gentry's existence.

Theodore and Mabel are sitting on the sofa in the parlor of their home as they hear the crunching of gravel under four tires and the hum of the V-8 engine pulling into the drive. Theodore pulls back the curtain to see the star decal along the side of a deputy sheriff's marked cruiser. The engine sounds quiet, and the driver's side door opens. Lawrence County Sheriff Deputy Charles Hauck has been a familiar face around Gentry Farm for six weeks. The sheriff's deputy removed his hat and walked toward the porch. Theodore meets the deputy at the top of the porch steps, and they quietly shake hands.

Finally, Charles breaks the silence by saying, "The sheriff has called off the search, Theo."

"So soon," Theodore replied with a hollow voice.

"There is nowhere else to look, and the county is running out of funds," says Deputy Hauck, avoiding Theodore's gaze and staring at the porch.

Meanwhile, Mabel overhears the conversation through the window. Expressionless and stoic, she stares straight ahead, void of any reaction to the news that nobody is looking for her daughter anymore.

There are no more tears to cry, no more hearts to break, and no more hope to hold onto. Mabel is hollow; a cold emptiness has eroded her foundation for faith, warmth, or purpose to remain. The threshold for her agony has reached its limit, and Mabel knows it is time to end the suffering. The weight of misery is more than she can bear.

It is almost 3:00 a.m. when Mabel walks out of her home, barefoot and wearing a nightgown. She walks down to the barn, looking for release. Mabel's heart begs for mercy from the misery of her heartache. She grabs a cattle rope hanging in the stable and climbs halfway up the loft ladder; she throws the rope over the rafters and ties a rudimentary knot. Mabel is unsavable and suffering. Without hesitation, she slips the rope over her head and takes her last step.

Mabel's body stiffens and jerks violently as her life force slips away. Everything fades to black; Mabel Gentry gives her soul back to God. Without her daughter and the light in her life, she has no use for it anymore.

Chapter Two

A moving truck pulls into Gentry Farm, carrying the furnishings and belongings the Tylers so carefully packed up in the days leading up to their fresh start and relocation. John Tyler and his wife, Emma, bring new optimism to Gentry Farm. Many buyers before them welcomed the challenge of restoration and rebirth only to abandon all efforts and hope, leaving hastily without notice to the realtors or the bank. John Tyler and his wife know nothing about the history of

Gentry Farm, and the realtors either want it that way or simply forgot.

John and Emma exit the moving truck and hug each other while staring at the old Victorian farmhouse. A sense of worthiness and determination overcomes John as he turns to Emma and says, "So, what do you think?"

"I think we've got our hands full," Emma replies.

"Well, maybe a little TLC and a lot of time and money will do it," John says.

"Time, we have; money is the problem," Emma chuckles.

"It won't be that bad, babe. I'm doing most of the work myself," John says, puffing out his chest with a proud smile.

"Oh Lord," Emma adds, laughing. John playfully chases Emma up the front walkway onto the porch. Life is finally starting to fall into place for the newlywed couple.

John is a slender man with sandy hair and blue eyes. He has a politician's smile and the bravado of a champion fighter. This attracted Emma to John two years ago when they first met at a co-worker's wedding in 2008. Emma was radiant in her bridesmaid's dress, and John couldn't stop staring at her. It took John all evening to walk up to the petite blonde with big green doe eyes and introduce himself. Emma hid it well, but she knew then that John Tyler had something she couldn't go without.

Opening the front door for the first time as the official property owners brought a flood of emotion to the newlywed couple. Excitement, wonder, joy, and accomplishment were some of the most profound. John and Emma walk through the old farmhouse, taking in the beautiful turn-of-the-century architecture. The twelve-foot-high ceilings with arched doorways and old ornate woodwork on the fireplace mantle transport them back to a much simpler time, a relic of history they are now the proud owners of.

Emma loved the vast cast-iron bathtub with lion's paw legs. She envisions many quiet, soothing soaks in the tub with the ambiance set just right, complete with an array of scented candles lit, bath bombs to soften her beautiful skin, and her favorite playlist of songs turned down low to calm her mind and lull her into relaxation.

Quickly, the daydreaming of victories to come is snatched away with the reminder of the monumental task of unloading the moving truck before nightfall. John and Emma ready themselves for labor as the heavy lifting begins. Since daylight hours are burning, John starts unloading the essential items to spend the first night in their new home. First to be unloaded is the California king-size bed with cherry wood head and footboards. This makes Emma and John rethink buying Amish hand-crafted furniture because a bill of sale with this furniture should come with a free consultation at the local chiropractor's office. Next come various essentials for the night, such as candles, since the electricity has not been turned on at the property. So, tonight will be spent just as the accommodation was when the house was built.

Emma starts unboxing cookware and assorted items as John carries in end tables, chairs, and picture frames. As the sun sets, a sense of adventure and wonderment sets in. John drives into town to pick up dinner as Emma places candles on all the sconces around the house. Emma notices how eerily quiet the farmhouse is outside of town, void of neighbors and the congestion of city life. It will take some getting used to, but with the new sense of isolation, a cold shiver runs up her spine.

When John arrives back at Gentry Farm, he finds his new home interior lit beautifully with the amber glow of a dozen candles. Emma even has candlesticks illuminating the kitchen table, complete with the table set with plates, silverware, and drinking glasses. John is taken aback by Emma's efficient use of time and can only mutter the word, "Wow."

"Tonight's theme is antiquity," Emma says as she takes the carryout bags from John's hands.

"I hope Lo Mein and General Tso's are okay," John says.

"Perfect," Emma answers.

"The options to choose from were limited in town," John chuckles.

"I've never had a candle-lit carry-out dinner before," Emma says.

"Well, tonight marks the beginning of several firsts," John boasts.

John and Emma seem happy and love-struck. They sit alone at the kitchen table and eat their first meal together in their new home as the night sets in and draws to a close.

John and Emma finish dinner, but discussions of renovation and restoration continue. Ideas for color schemes and interior design go long into the night. John's ideas for stripping and sanding the hardwood floors and all the ornate woodwork seem to be a sure thing, but other ideas for his private study are less popular with Emma. She has plans for a nursery soon instead.

John and Emma clean up after dinner and begin to get ready for bed. The temperature seems to have dropped quickly as John comments on gathering firewood for the fireplace. Emma pulls her cardigan tight around her while carrying a candlestick towards the upstairs master bedroom. The same shiver she had earlier runs up Emma's spine as she reaches the top of the staircase. She notices her breath is visible as every lit candle in the house blows out in unison. Pitch black shrouds the house, and Emma calls for John to bring matches as she feels a presence, but it is not John's.

"John, is that you?" Emma cries out.

"I am coming, honey!" John says.

"Somebody is up here, John," she adds.

"Don't be silly. I'm on my way, babe," John replies. John makes his way to the top of the staircase while striking a match. "Here you go, honey," John says.

"It got so cold quickly, and every candle went out simultaneously!" Emma explains.

"I know, creepy, right?" John snickers.

"No, I'm serious. I felt like somebody was up here!" Emma says.

"This house is just old and drafty, honey. That's why it got cold, and all the candles went out at once. Just a draft, Emma, nothing to get the willies over," John explains.

Emma accepts the logical explanation, and they go to bed. They make love as always, which seems much needed for the stress relief of the day, before quickly drifting off to sleep soon after.

Chapter Three

A week has passed since the Tylers spent their first night on Gentry Farm, and they finally feel acclimated to their unfamiliar environment. Moving in is complete, and John starts preparing to restore the old Victorian farmhouse. John has the tailgate of his truck down and his toolbox sitting on it as he starts to take inventory of all the tools he will need before getting started. Power drills and power sanders are going to be essential, he thinks to himself, as well as a reciprocating saw, hammer, and measuring tape.

John's focus is broken by an old, rattly truck lumbering down the gravel driveway. The driver of the truck looks familiar to John. The old Dodge rolls to a squeaky stop, and an older man in his mid-sixties slowly opens the driver's door and steps out. The man has a meandering swagger, and you can tell at first sight that he is as rough as a Brillo pad. Broad-shouldered, with arms like tree trunks, he wears a dusty tan cowboy hat, a short-sleeved button-up shirt halfway buttoned, and cowboy boots with one denim pant leg tucked half into his boot and the other pant leg over his boot.

The visitor and John approach each other as the man speaks first.

"Good morning, young man."

"Good morning, sir," John replies as they shake hands. John notices his hands are heavy and calloused. He has a certain stature and demeanor as if he is looking down on you, even though John is about an inch taller than the man.

"I see you are getting settled in. My name is R.C., but everyone calls me Bunk," says the man.

"Nice to meet you, Bunk. I am John Tyler," John replies.

"I own the horse farm just down the road. I wanted to introduce myself and see if you need help getting situated," Bunk says.

"Well, I appreciate that, sir. It means a lot," John answers.

"Call me Bunk, I am no sir," Bunk counters.

"Okay, Bunk, as of right now, I seem to have things under control, but if I do need help, I'd be much obliged to you for doing so," says John.

"Anytime, young man. Let me ask you a question," Bunk says.

"Sure," John adds.

"What made you decide to lay down roots at Gentry Farm?" Bunk asks.

"It seemed like a great prospect to turn into a home and start a family, plus the bank and realtors had a good deal on the place," John answers.

"Did they happen to tell you the history of the farm?" Bunk asks.

"They did not," John says. Bunk's stern brow raises with curiosity.

John listens in stunned silence as Bunk tells how little Meredith Gentry went missing from the farm in 1967. Bunk explained that he was a young man at the time and was part of the search party that looked for Meredith for six weeks with no luck. Then, when Bunk told John the grief was too much for Mabel Gentry to bear, and she hung herself in the barn, John's blood ran cold.

"So, it seems a dark cloud has hung over the farm ever since," Bunk says.

"Is that why the farm had such a great price?" John asks.

"Maybe so. This place has been bought and sold several times over the years. Nobody stays long," Bunk says.

John says nothing, but his thoughts are racing from the weight of the history of Gentry

Farm. How does he tell Emma about this? Or does he tell her at all? John has a lot to think about, let alone process and make peace with.

John and Bunk shake hands, and his new neighbor returns to his truck.

"And one last thing, young man," Bunk says.

"What's that?" John replies.

"She is going to test your faith. You are a man of faith, aren't you?" Bunk asks with a concerned gaze.

"I am, and who is she?" John replies.

Bunk says nothing else as he climbs into his truck and turns over the engine. The truck slowly ambles down the gravel driveway, kicking up dust.

John's focus shifts away from restoration, and he's preoccupied with the past for the rest of the day. Bunk's words weigh heavily on John's mind and chest throughout the evening. Emma is so content and optimistic about their new location and the enduring spirit of hope she brings with her that John doesn't see the need or have the heart to tell her about the history of Gentry Farm. For the first time in their relationship, and with a guilty conscience, John starts keeping a secret from his wife.

The day draws to a close with dinner and drinks by the fireplace. The popping and snapping of the glowing red embers lull the couple into complete relaxation. Within minutes, the couple's silence is accompanied by sleep. John and Emma Tyler spend the rest of the evening warm and comfortable, asleep on the couch before the fireplace.

Chapter Four

Emma Tyler's to-do list is never fully complete. Some tasks get marked off, and the list gets shorter, but more tasks get added without fail, and the cycle continues. Today's to-do list has several chores that Emma plans to do while running errands in town. To "kill two birds with one stone" sounds macabre but is somehow fitting.

It is a little after 9:00 a.m. when Emma climbs into her Malibu and makes her way up the gravel driveway of Gentry Farm. The weather is ideal today for driving with the windows down and taking in the sights and smells of her new home. Emma's car fills with the scent of honeysuckle and blackberry bushes, and the crunch of the gravel under her tires reminds her that the road less traveled can be picturesque and serene.

Emma's first stop along her way to complete her daily chores is to stop by the bank and make a payment on her installment loan. The drive-through at the bank seems to be the quickest and most efficient way to mark the first task off her list, so Emma waits in the drive-through line and touches up her lipstick in the rear-view mirror. Maroon 5 plays on the radio while she gently pulls up to the teller's window. The errand is complete within a few minutes, and Emma is off to her next destination. Just a couple of miles down the road from the bank, Emma pulls into the parking lot of the local supercenter to shop for some groceries and various sundries. Emma quickly fills her cart with the needed items and heads to the self-checkout aisle. Grocery shopping is Emma's least favorite task, and she tries her best to complete it as quickly as possible.

The last stop of the day for Emma is the gas station, where she fills her car with gasoline and buys a couple of scratch-off lottery tickets. The lottery tickets are Emma's secret slight addiction. Although harmless, she thinks that stopping the urge to play the lottery would be challenging. Emma makes her way back home before the afternoon is over. John is busy replacing shutters and gutters on the house, so Emma starts carrying bags of groceries and the items recently bought at the store. The job takes four trips, but Emma finally completes her to-do list for the day, except for putting all the items away.

You're in the final stretch now, Emma thinks to herself. First, she puts away the frozen foods and dairy products. Then, she refrigerates all the other items. The canned goods are quickly stored in the cabinets. Finally, she places all the hygiene items and cleaning supplies in their proper spots. Emma almost forgets about the most essential item. She feels lucky that John didn't walk inside and see it before she could hide it. Emma takes the pregnancy test from the bottom of the bag and quickly hides it in her purse. Emma looks deep in concentration as she thinks she wants to be sure to pick the right time to tell John if she is pregnant, but women know these things and she's almost sure she is. So, for the first time in her marriage, Emma has a secret she is keeping from John.

The rest of the day passes quickly, and before John and Emma realize it, evening has set in. Emma prepares a quick dinner of chicken cutlets and steamed vegetables. As they eat dinner by the fireplace, John breaks the silence by telling Emma about his day. Emma laughs at the thought of John doing restoration work because she has never known John to do any carpentry work. Emma thinks she learns something new about her husband daily.

Emma prepares for the next day by updating her to-do list and putting away folded laundry. Carrying folded towels to the bathroom upstairs, Emma notices the lights in the chandelier down the hallway flickering. Emma stops, staring at the chandelier, when she feels an ominous and creepy feeling overcome her. The hair on the nape of Emma's neck stands on end. Emma's breath becomes visible as the temperature drops thirty degrees instantly. She wants to scream with panic and fear, but no sounds escape her. Genuine fear paralyzes her.

Standing directly behind Emma in the hallway is the disembodied soul of Mabel Gentry. The tortured specter's face is shrouded with coal-black hair, her neck is slightly stretched, and her skin is ashen white. Mabel is as solid in appearance as you and me. She rips and tears at her white nightgown as if she has never lost the misery that ended her life so many years ago. Emma shakes off the paralysis that had its grip on her as she spins around to find nobody standing behind her. Emma cries out to John with a particular anguish in her voice that brings John running. "What's wrong, honey? Are you okay?" John asks. "I don't know, the lights started flickering, and it got cold! I was overwhelmed with sadness," Emma starts to cry as John holds her and tells her everything is okay. "I'll look at the lights tomorrow, probably just a short in the wiring," John says. "No, that's not the point. Something is going on in this house,

John," Emma exclaims. John tries to downplay what just happened and gives half-hearted and weak explanations, but just below the surface of John's excuses, he knows who and what is to blame.

Chapter Five

A murder of crows inhabits a dead oak tree on Gentry Farm, and a full harvest moon lights the backdrop of the deep purple sky. The crows have been the unofficial caretakers of the property for some time now. An early morning fog crawls slowly across the ground, shrouding every step toward the old Victorian farmhouse. It is 4:00 a.m., and John Tyler's peaceful slumber is infected and disturbed by nightmares.

John kicks and thrashes in his sleep from a recurring nightmare that has plagued his subconscious since he made Gentry Farm his new home. John is sweating and breathing heavily as he cries out, "No, please stop," from flash images of Mabel Gentry swinging from her neck, arm stretched out, and empty black eyes piercing deep into John's soul. Mabel is reaching out for John, her mouth open but absent of any voice as her purple and lifeless lips try to say the words, help me. John cannot run or avoid the vivid imagery that haunts his sleep. His body moves as if it is trapped in quicksand as the swinging corpse that was once Mabel Gentry reaches closer and closer. "No, leave me alone!" John screams aloud.

"John, are you okay? John, wake up." Emma shakes John violently. John awakens abruptly in a panic. A moment passes before he realizes he was dreaming and is safe in bed with his beautiful wife. A calming relief starts to relax John as he lays his head back on his pillow and tells Emma he is okay and was having a nightmare.

When Emma does not comment or comfort John with any soothing words, John looks over to his wife. Instead of Emma lying directly beside him, it is the icy chill of the black eyes of the entity that was once Mabel

Gentry. Nose to nose, John tries to scream in horror, only to feel his lungs paralyzed in terror. Panic-stricken and traumatized, John awakes fully from his nightmare and sits straight up, screaming in horror.

Some revelations come to you like a whisper in the wind, and others strike you like a lightning bolt. The revelation that John and Emma's new home is haunted hits John Tyler so profoundly that the words of his neighbor, Bunk, carry so much weight and clarity that John's entire world is in disarray. Like a vinyl record player, Bunk's words keep playing in John's head repeatedly. She will test your faith. Only at this moment did John know exactly what Bunk was telling him.

Emma is ripped from her sleep by John screaming. "John, are you okay? What is wrong?"

"Just a nightmare, I'm sorry," John replies. He puts his feet on the floor and his face in his hands. His labored breathing starts to slow, and John walks to the bathroom to splash water on his face. Emma is left sitting in bed, confused, and her mind races over John's scary episode.

As John turns the faucet on to wash away the uneasiness and fright he has just experienced, he knows there is no denying or hiding what he believes is evident in his home. John walks out of the bathroom and back into the bedroom, drying his face with a hand towel. He stands in front of Emma, still sitting in bed, hesitating to speak because he fears how the words might sound aloud.

"Our house is haunted, Emma," John says bluntly and to the point.

"What, are you serious?" Emma scoffs at the notion.

"You know it too, honey. You don't want to believe it. When I met our neighbor last week, he alluded to the fact that this house has a dark cloud over it, and no owner has ever lived here long. After he told me the history of this farm, I can see why," John says.

"What is the history of this farm, John? Why haven't you told me any of this?" Emma asks.

"I didn't want to scare you or let anything mess up our plans, honey," John answers.

"Tell me, John, what's wrong with our house?" Emma exclaims.

John recants the history of Gentry Farm as told to him by his neighbor, Bunk. Emma listens in amazement and horror. When John finishes with the disturbing account on their property, Emma has tears rolling down her cheeks. She is unsure if the sadness and despair staining Gentry Farm brings her to tears or the realization of the picturesque and fairytale-like perception she had of her new home being destroyed and infected with this horror story-like past and present reputation.

Emma is speechless. The thought of sleep is lost for the rest of the night. She gets up, puts the coffee on, and takes a shower. Emma sits quietly at the kitchen table, drinking coffee and staring out the windows as the sun breaks over the horizon, marking the end of one of the most uneasy and horrendous nights that Emma can ever remember.

John joins her in the kitchen, fills up his coffee cup, and sits at the kitchen table with Emma. Neither speaks at first, but Emma breaks the silence by saying, "Well, you are right, John. I knew something was different about this house from our first night here. I didn't want to believe it, but I felt it. I know she is here," Emma says.

John reaches across the table and holds Emma's hand. "I guess there is not a good time to tell you, so I'll tell you now," Emma says softly.

"Okay, what is it?" John asks.

"I'm pregnant, John," Emma answers as she begins to cry.

Chapter Six

Emma's reaction from John was not what she had always envisioned or anticipated when she told him she was pregnant. Emma had always dreamed of the shocked look or excitement on his face, or at least an outpouring of positive emotion, but she got neither of those things that a mother-to-be always hopes for. John remained silent and wore a mask of concern and confusion as he tried to process the news the morning had brought him.

Emma storms to the bathroom and slams the door as she cries hysterically because the emotional overload is more than she can take. "I'm sorry, Emma, I'm just shocked, that's all," John says through the bathroom door.

"Just go away. I want to be alone!" Emma cries out.

"Listen, I'm happy, baby. It has just been a messed-up morning! I was not expecting that. I love you, Emma!" John pleads with his forehead leaning against the bathroom door.

"Today should be one of the best days of our lives, John! Instead, I am terrified and heartbroken. Please leave me alone!" Emma sobs.

John walks away from the bathroom slowly, head hung in defeat. At this moment, the happy and positive energy that John and Emma bring to the farm is fleeting, and the ominous and gloomy vibe that infests the farm starts to reflect in Tyler's marriage and everyday life. The only way John knows how to deal with stress and anxiety is to work. He puts on his work boots, grabs his toolbox, and heads out the door. There is work to be done to the old prairie barn, and John knows the labor will help him decompress and reflect on his current unforeseen situation.

Emma is still trying to gather herself and wrap her mind around her plight in the bathroom. With red puffy eyes and a running nose, Emma looks at herself in the mirror and thinks she looks terrible. It's time to change out of her nightgown and into her clothes for the day, but first, she washes her face and starts brushing her teeth. Quietly and distantly, Emma hears her name whispered ever so softly. Uncertain of whether Emma had just heard her name, she turns off the faucet, and with her toothbrush still in her mouth, she looks behind the shower curtain and finds nothing. When she looks back at the mirror above the bathroom sink, her blood runs cold, and paralysis overcomes her body. Instead of her reflection, Emma is looking eye to eye at the ghostly apparition of Mabel Gentry.

Mabel's hair is long and dark, masking her face slightly. The complexion of the lost spirit has the ashen greyness of death. Mabel's eyes are deep and empty of any life. Emma is stuck in frightened silence for what seems like an eternity. Mabel's blank and emotionless stare cuts through Emma's bravery and convictions like a knife. She explodes out the bathroom door, nearly breaking the door hinges with her exit. Frantic and terrified, Emma sprints down the stairs, screaming for John. She looks in the kitchen and the living room. Finally, Emma bolts out the front door onto the porch and calls John's name.

Emma's cries of distress for her husband carry to the barn, which sits about a hundred yards away from the house. John hears Emma scream his name, immediately registers the panic in her voice, and starts a full-paced sprint towards Emma. When John reaches the house, he finds Emma sitting on the front porch, rocking back and forth and crying uncontrollably.

"What's wrong, Emma? Talk to me, please!" John pleads.

"I saw her, John! I saw the ghost! It was horrible!" Emma sobs as John hugs her.

"Where? Where did you see her?" John asks.

"In the bathroom! She was in the mirror!" Emma replies.

John can only hold her, and for a moment, any soothing words of comfort elude him.

John helps Emma to her feet and holds her hand as they walk into the living room and sit on the couch. Emma dries her eyes and tries to pull herself together as she tells John, "I'm pregnant, John. There is no way I'm raising this child in a haunted house."

"I don't know how to make her leave, honey," John says softly.

"Either she leaves, or we will, John!" Emma snaps.

Right then, Bunk's words come flooding into John's memory like an epiphany. Many people have bought this place over the years, but none stay long.

"We can't get out of the house and property agreement without losing a lot of money, Emma," John explains.

"We can't live like this, John!" Emma says.

"I know honey, I will fix it, I promise. It's not good for you or the baby to get this upset," says John.

"I know it's not. I'm going to my mom's house for the day to relax and calm down. I'll be back tonight," Emma says.

There was no debating or rebuttal from John, and with that, Emma gathered a few things she would need for the day, loaded them into her car, and left the terrifying ordeal and the stress of it at Gentry Farm. A weight was lifted off Emma's shoulders as soon as she left the property.

John Tyler sits on the steps of his old Victorian farmhouse, drowning in defeat and confusion. John is in deep concentration, trying to think of a solution or a way out. How could he explain to anyone that they gave up their dream and home with a baby on the way because the place is haunted? That sounds ridiculous, John thinks to himself.

Remembering he was about to start a restoration project on the barn, John began to walk back to grab his toolbox. In broad daylight, with a clear line of sight, John sees a solid figure of a woman with long dark hair in a nightgown standing in the open doorway of the barn. This was the same woman from his dreams, he thought to himself. This must be Mabel. She stands expressionless with one arm outstretched, pointing into the barn.

It is not fear that overcomes John Tyler upon seeing the ghost of Gentry Farm. It is anger and rage that overtakes him. John screams at her, "What do you want? We're not leaving! I'm not afraid of you!" John knew this was a lie because behind the mask of rage lies an abundance of fear. The solid apparition of Mabel Gentry slowly begins to fade away into the open space like an old memory. John notices his hands trembling and his heart pounding like a drum at the profound realization of his haunted home.

Chapter Seven

By the time 9:30 p.m. rolled around and Emma still had not come home, John grew worried. He called Emma's cell phone, and she did not answer. John tries to ease his concern by running plausible scenarios through his mind and not rushing to judgment. At 10:50 p.m. John calls Emma's phone again, and this time, she answers. He is relieved she is okay and starts the conversation tentatively. "Hey honey, are you okay?" John asks.

"I don't know, John. I'm just confused and scared," Emma answers.

"I know, honey. I'm going to fix this, I promise," John replies.

"How, John? What can we do?" Emma asks.

"I've been thinking we need some help from somebody who knows how to deal with this stuff," John answers.

"You mean like a psychic?" Emma asks.

"Yes, like a psychic. The only problem is I have no idea where to look for one," John answers.

"I think I might know. My Aunt Ruth is a medium. Her whole life, she has claimed to talk to the other side. I can call her and see if she can help us," Emma explains.

"That's a good idea. Are you coming home tonight?" John asks.

"It's too late now. I'll call Aunt Ruth in the morning, and then I'll be home, I promise," Emma answers.

The following day came quickly, and Emma was up with the sun. She made the bed in her mother's spare bedroom, where she had slept, and dressed for the day before coming downstairs to smell freshly brewed coffee and bacon frying in the cast-iron skillet on the stove. The bacon sizzling and popping made for a familiar background noise as Emma sat at the kitchen table while her mother prepared breakfast.

Emma's mother, Rosalyn, is a petite lady with salt-and-pepper hair pulled back into a ponytail. Large golden hoop earrings match her necklace and watch that Emma bought her for Christmas the year prior. Rosalyn is humming her favorite church hymn this morning and seems happy to have her only daughter back home, if only briefly.

"Good morning, Mom," Emma says cheerfully.

"Good morning, baby. How did you sleep?" Rosalyn replies.

"I slept great. Before I go home, I want to talk to Aunt Ruth. It has been a while since we spoke, and I want to catch up," says Emma.

"That's a great idea. You should give her a call. I want to see how long it takes her to sense you're pregnant," Rosalyn replies.

"Do you think she will know?" Emma asks.

"Yes, your Aunt Ruth has a sense for these things," Rosalyn smirks.

Emma's mother writes down Aunt Ruth's number before setting Emma's plate on the table and joining her with only a cup of coffee for herself.

"Eat up, honey. You are eating for two," Rosalyn says with a warm and motherly smile.

"Thank you, Mom. It looks great," Emma says.

After Emma finishes her breakfast and clears the kitchen table, she pulls out her cell phone, dials Aunt Ruth's number, and anxiously waits for her to answer.

"Hello," a soft voice comes through after three rings.

"Hi, Aunt Ruth, it's Emma. How are you?" Emma asks.

"Oh, I'm great, darling. How far along are you?" asks Ruth.

"What do you mean?" Emma replies with a look of stunned amazement on her face.

"You're pregnant, dear. How far along are you?" Ruth asks again.

"I don't know. I just found out," replies Emma.

The conversation continues with small talk, and then Emma tells Ruth about Gentry Farm.

"I better visit your new home, dear. I think my visit could be most helpful to your situation. How about this weekend?" Ruth suggests.

"Thank you so much, Aunt Ruth. This weekend would be great," replies Emma with a sigh of relief.

Emma gives Aunt Ruth her address and tells her that any time in the evening would be fine.

"I will see you this weekend, Aunt Ruth. I love you," Emma says.

"I love you too, darling," replies Ruth.

They both hang up the phone, and Emma feels a weight lifted off her shoulders. Aunt Ruth has a way of making any problem seem manageable.

Emma gathers her belongings and places them neatly in her overnight bag. She checks her hair and makeup in the mirror before returning downstairs to search for her mother.

"Thank you, Mom. I love you," says Emma as she bids her farewell.

"I love you too, honey. Did you talk to your Aunt Ruth?" Rosalyn asks.

"I did. It was so good to talk to her. She knew immediately and asked me how far along I was," Emma chuckles.

"I knew she would," Rosalyn replies.

After their goodbyes, Emma loads her overnight bag and purse into her car, waves at her mother on the porch, and returns home to Gentry Farm. Just the thought of going back there makes Emma nauseous with dread, or could it be the morning sickness she is experiencing?

As Emma makes her way down the long gravel driveway at Gentry Farm, she notices John up on a ladder, painting the ornate woodwork on the eaves of the front porch an off-white or eggshell color.

"Hey, John," Emma calls out.

John notices Emma is home and hurries down the ladder with a sense of urgency like a child on Christmas morning.

Emma climbs out of her car and into a long embrace from John that seems to last forever.

"I was only gone a day, John," Emma says as she hugs John back.

"I know, but it was a day too long," John replies.

John carries Emma's overnight bag up the walkway for her as they make their way inside. Emma tells John about the phone call with Aunt Ruth and her visit to the farm this weekend. John feels optimistic as the two sit and reflect on the couch.

Chapter Eight

As autumn draws closer, fall colors start to overtake Gentry Farm. The leaves are turning gold and auburn as the days grow shorter. A brisk evening breeze sweeps over the property, carrying the scents of the harvesting lands nearby. As Saturday evening inches closer and the sun starts to set in the west, beautiful pinks and oranges paint the sky against a backdrop of grey clouds, signaling the day's end.

At 6:45 p.m., the sound of tires rolling over gravel grabs Emma's attention as she finishes washing dishes. She knows her Aunt Ruth has arrived. Emma hollers up the stairs to John that Aunt Ruth is here. Drying her hands, she heads to the front porch. John makes his way down the staircase and joins Emma on the porch. The driver's door of a black Jeep opens, and Aunt Ruth steps out, wearing a radiant smile.

Ruth is a petite, elegantly dressed lady in a black cardigan over a white blouse and black capri pants. Her short hair is salon-perfect, and as Emma hugs her, the scent of Chanel fills her senses. "I'm so glad you're here, Aunt Ruth.

I've missed you!" Emma exclaims. "I'm thrilled to be here, honey! Where is this handsome man I've heard so much about?" Ruth replies. "Aunt Ruth, this is my husband, John," Emma introduces. After hugging Aunt Ruth, John welcomes her into the house. Before heading up the walkway, takes time to stop and look at the old Victorian farmhouse for a moment.

"This is such a beautiful house, Emma, with such a sad and heartbreaking past," Ruth comments, taking Emma's hand as they follow John inside. Emma shows Aunt Ruth around, discussing renovation plans and home décor ideas. Impressed with the old Victorian home,

Aunt Ruth listens as Emma explains their troubles with the house and the sighting of Mabel's apparition in the mirror. Emma's eyes well up with tears as she talks about the stress and burden the farm has placed on them.

Aunt Ruth believes she can help and senses the sadness in the energy of Gentry Farm. "I want to try and contact Mabel's spirit. She needs help moving toward the other side," Aunt Ruth states. "How do we do that?" Emma asks. "We'll have a séance, darling. I'll ask her to speak with us and find out why she's here," Aunt Ruth explains. Initially reluctant, Emma trusts her Aunt Ruth's expertise and agrees to the séance, hoping it will bring clarity and answers.

Aunt Ruth instructs John and Emma to remain quiet as she clears her mind, focuses on her breathing, and enters a meditative state. This relaxed and open-minded state will serve as the conduit through which Ruth attempts to communicate with any entities willing to talk.

Emma turns off the lights and TV in the house, then lights the candles in the sconces on the fireplace mantle and the candlestick holders on the kitchen table. The flickering candlelight casts an ominous yet serene atmosphere, filling John and Emma with a sense of anxiety and concern.

Aunt Ruth tells John and Emma to sit at the kitchen table and hold hands as she tries to enter a clairvoyant state. The candlelight casts three shadows on the wall—Emma, John, and Aunt Ruth—all holding hands. Ruth closes her eyes and starts taking deep, steady breaths until she looks relaxed and at peace. Suddenly, her chest heaves upward rapidly, and a long groan escapes her. Emma exchanges a surprised and worried glance with John as Ruth begins to summon any entity that might be present. "Who is in this room with us?" Ruth asks aloud. The candles flicker, and the room's temperature drops, making their breath visible.

Disembodied whispers, multiple voices at once, flood the room, seeming to come from everywhere and nowhere simultaneously. Ruth's head droops, and a voice unlike her own erupts across the table, loud and terrifying. "This is my house," it declares. Emma wants to speak, to ask Aunt Ruth if she's okay, but no words come out. "Who are you?" John demands. "I want my baby. Please help me!" The voice strains as it leaves Ruth's body.

A shadowy figure looms behind John. An icy chill runs up his spine, his breathing becomes rapid and labored, and flash images flood his mind—visions of a horse stomping the ground and a shovel in a mound of dirt. The sounds of the spade stabbing the earth and the horse's distress fill John's mind. Tears roll down Emma's face as she watches John's torment. The grief that Mabel endured in her final moments has mentally, emotionally, and physically worn John down. He collapses on the kitchen floor.

Chapter Nine

John Tyler awakens in a state of confusion. Aunt Ruth and Emma surround him, their faces filled with concern and worry. Emma holds his hand, sobbing. "John, are you okay? Please talk to me!" she pleads. "I'm okay. I just got lightheaded," John reassures her. "This was a bad idea, Aunt Ruth. I'm sorry," Emma admits. "No, it needed to be done, my dear," Aunt Ruth insists. They help John to his feet, and he slowly ascends the creaky old staircase. Each step groans and squeaks under his weight as John rubs his forehead, trying to gather his senses. With each step becoming more laborious than the last, John looks up and is horrified to see a ghostly silhouette of the apparition that has haunted his dreams and farm. Mabel Gentry's specter is in torment, tearing at her hair and nightgown in agony. John lets out a blood-curdling scream that seems to catch Mabel's attention. She gazes at him through her long, black hair with hollow, empty eyes and points past John toward the barn, where she took her final steps. Aunt Ruth and Emma rush up the staircase to John's aid.

In an instant, the ghost of Mabel vanishes, leaving John in emotional turmoil. "We have to listen to what she's telling us," Aunt Ruth insists. "I'm listening. I don't know what she's saying," John replies. "Push past the fear, resist the urge to run from her, and listen. She's here because she needs your help, darling," Aunt Ruth urges. "She's looking for her baby," Emma states calmly and matter-of-factly.

Both John and Emma are exhausted from the emotional and physical toll of the night. It's too late for Aunt Ruth to drive home, so Emma insists she stay until morning. "Thank you so much, darling; I hate to impose," Aunt Ruth says. "No imposition at all. You're family, and I love you. Plus, it's been too long, Aunt Ruth. We need this time to catch up and reconnect," Emma replies sympathetically. "I love you, Emma," Aunt Ruth responds.

Emma retrieves extra blankets and sheets from the chest of drawers, preparing the guest room for Aunt Ruth. As Aunt Ruth settles in for the night, she's drawn to the window overlooking the farm. A sense of heartache, secrecy, and sorrow fills her as she contemplates the sinister events that might have trapped Mabel Gentry's spirit. How does a soul become so tormented, unable to find rest?

The night falls, with a crescent moon paired with sparkling stars, resembling diamonds on black velvet. A murder of crows takes the night watch in the bare oak tree's limbs, sitting stoically like gargoyles atop a gothic cathedral. Aunt Ruth, feeling weary, knows her slumber will be restless.

In the guest bedroom, Ruth switches off the nightstand lamp, plunging the room into darkness. Outside, the wind howls, and small cyclones spin dead leaves on the ground, suggesting an unsettling energy about the property. As Ruth drifts into sleep, her dreams are invaded by flash images of violence and terror—screams, breaking glass, shadows of Theo Gentry striking Mabel, feelings of fear and sadness. She tosses and turns, crying out in her sleep, "Stop!" Domestic violence sounds flood her dreams, and a baby's cries jolt her awake. Heart pounding and breathing rapidly, Ruth sits up and exclaims, "That son of a bitch killed the baby!"

Unable to sleep further, Ruth checks the wall clock—it's 3:00 a.m., the witching hour. Still in her nightclothes, she descends the stairs, haunted by the horrifying images of baby Meredith's final moments.

Ruth starts the coffee pot, attempting to calm her mind, but the disturbing scenes from her dreams replay like an old victrola record player. Sensitive to the negative and sorrowful energy, she feels emotionally drained. Theo Gentry, in a drunken rage, not only abused

Mabel but also killed the toddler for crying too much, Ruth concludes. Overwhelmed by the atrocity, Ruth quietly weeps.

The dawn breaks on the horizon with a beautiful amber glow. Frost has blanketed the farm overnight, and the low temperature signals that winter is fast approaching. With the days growing shorter, a gloomy vibe pervades the farm, suggesting a contentment with the ever-present darkness. John and Emma descend the stairs to begin their morning and are surprised to find breakfast already prepared, with Aunt Ruth sitting at the kitchen table, sipping coffee. "Good morning, darling," Aunt Ruth greets. "Good morning," John and Emma respond in unison.

They sit in stunned silence as Aunt Ruth recounts a profound epiphany about what happened to baby Meredith. John and Emma now understand why Mabel remains and what she is asking of them.

Chapter Ten

Aunt Ruth's departure is solemn and heartfelt. Emma hugs her aunt tightly for a few extra moments. "I love you, Aunt Ruth," Emma says. "I love you too, darling. I'm so proud of you, and I can't wait to meet your beautiful baby girl," Aunt Ruth replies. John and Emma exchange shocked and excited glances. Having learned not to doubt Aunt Ruth, Emma's eyes fill with tears as she asks, "I'm having a little girl?" "Yes, a beautiful, healthy, green-eyed angel. She looks just like her mother when she was little," Aunt Ruth confirms.

John's face shows surprise, joy, and wonder as he hugs Aunt Ruth goodbye. As they part, she whispers in John's ear, "Do not worry; this too shall pass. You know what you must do, besides looking after my most amazing and beautiful niece!" "Yes, ma'am, I promise," John replies quietly. "Don't be afraid of her, dear. Listen to her," Aunt Ruth adds. With that, she slides on her Dolce & Gabbana sunglasses, gracefully gets into her vehicle, and slowly drives away, leaving Gentry Farm in her rear-view mirror.

On her drive home through the back roads of the foothills of the Appalachian Mountains, Aunt Ruth marvels at the beauty of Southern Ohio in autumn. The landscape is painted with the vibrant colors of harvest time—vivid oranges and crimson leaves dotting golden mazes and hunter greens. Deer graze in pastures along the scenic route to Haver Hill, Ohio. Aunt Ruth takes this quiet, therapeutic drive as an opportunity to pray—for the lost soul of Mabel Gentry and for clarity and strength for John and Emma during this challenging time.

Reflecting on the emotionally taxing twenty-four hours she has just experienced,

Aunt Ruth feels a sense of relief. A heavy burden has been lifted, allowing her to breathe freely. She feels that God is removing all her worries and transgressions from her heart, as He always has. In that moment, she knows that not only are John and Emma enveloped in divine truth and protected by God's glory, but also that the souls of Mabel and Meredith Gentry will soon join hands and find peace in the Kingdom of Heaven. By the time she arrives home, Aunt Ruth has found balance and peace within herself.

John and Emma are overwhelmed with emotions and questions following Aunt Ruth's visit. As much as they cherished their time with her, the visit feels bittersweet to the Tylers. On one hand, they find the séance frightening and detrimental to John; on the other hand, they now understand why the ghost of Mabel Gentry haunts both the farm and their lives.

Emma runs a hot bath upstairs to unwind and soak away the day's stresses. John grabs a Michelob bottle from the fridge and builds a fire in the fireplace using chopped wood he had cut himself from a dead poplar tree on the property.

As Emma listens to "Stay" by Sugarland on her playlist, she lights candles in the main bathroom and drops two bath bombs into the bathwater. A quiet, peaceful, therapeutic evening is long overdue. Emma dips her fingertips into the bathwater to check the temperature. At the same time, she hears small scampering footsteps outside the main bathroom in the hallway. The pitter-patter of a child's footsteps causes Emma to question her initial interpretation of the noise. "John, what are you doing?" Emma calls out. She receives no response from John, but instead, hears a playful giggle down the hallway, followed by more scampering footsteps. Emma puts her bathrobe back on and slowly opens the bathroom door. She peeks into the hallway, hesitant and curious. Looking towards the main bedroom, she sees nothing. Suddenly, she hears the playful giggling right beside her ear. In slow motion, she turns her head towards the staircase.

At the top of the old Victorian home's staircase stands the most adorable and saddest little girl Emma has ever seen. Her breath catches, and she stands frozen in astonishment at the sight of this beautiful toddler. The little girl appears so sad and lonely that Emma feels the energy permeate the hallway and into her body, immediately bringing tears of sorrow to her eyes. The toddler looks as solid and alive as anyone else. Her black curly locks fall perfectly to her shoulders. The rosiest, puffy cheeks frame lips in a slight pout, attempting to hold back a whimper. She wears an adorable blue and white sundress with a bow tied at the back. A matching blue bow adorns her hair, and the most emerald, green doe eyes lock onto Emma's, seemingly saying hello.

Emma is struck by her visitor at the top of the stairs. Tears roll down her cheeks as she takes the smallest, slowest steps toward the little girl. With her heart pounding and mind racing, she tries to rationalize who this could be and how she ended up at the top of her staircase. Emma's powers of deduction work overtime as she tries to convince herself that this little girl is someone other than who her heart and mind recognize her to be.

Taking another small step towards the little girl, Emma finally regains her ability to speak. She manages to whisper, "How are you? You must be Meredith." The little girl remains still and silent, but her emerald green eyes convey everything Emma needs to know. Another step brings Emma so close that she bends down at the waist and extends her hands to Meredith. "Come here, honey, it's okay," Emma says softly. Meredith's small hands reach up to Emma, seeking love, salvation, and safety. When Emma's hands touch Meredith's, the beautiful illusion shatters into a horrific nightmare. The once radiant and beautiful little girl transforms into the decomposing, lifeless, and terrifying corpse of Meredith Gentry. Hollow, sunken, empty black eyes replace the once gorgeous emerald green eyes, and the corpse's complexion turns bluish-gray, splitting open.

There is flesh on the entity's hands and lower jaw. Emma lets out the most primal scream ever heard. The jawbone of the apparition falls off the skull, and the entire body of the specter crumbles and rots in Emma's hands. She drops to her knees, screaming and desperately crawling backward in retreat. John comes running up the stairs in total panic. The ghostly toddler fades away, leaving Emma inconsolable against the wall, wailing in pure terror and misery. John is unable to comfort her the entire night. Emma is left emotionally and spiritually broken, curled up in the fetal position in her bed. "God, please be with Emma Tyler tonight."

Chapter Eleven

John is in a state of confusion and peril. He has no idea what Emma just experienced or how to help her. Emma refuses to talk about it, only crying and praying under her breath. The ghostly and grim spectacle that this farm presents on a routine basis is spiritually and emotionally draining for John and Emma, and any hope for relief seems bleak.

The fire in the fireplace is extinguished, and the remaining Michelob is poured down the sink. The lights downstairs are switched off, the doors locked, marking the end of a defeated evening and extinguishing any hope for a peaceful and soothing night.

Emma's husband climbs into bed with her and turns off the nightstand lamp, plunging the room into complete darkness. The house is eerily quiet on this night; only the sounds of crickets can be heard, no rustling of dead leaves. Only John's breathing is audible, as if the house itself stalks John and Emma with a silent, menacing intention. It doesn't take long for John to drift off into sleep. The Tylers are beginning to lose their grip on their rational well-being, their mental health, and even their home. Thus, it's no surprise when the sandman releases a torrent of all-too-familiar night terrors: flash images clustered randomly in John's subconscious mind. Frightened mares and steeds hysterically stomp the earth, rearing up on hindquarters in panic, and clumsy beasts of burden are distraught with strain and stress. A bassinet filled to the top with earthworms and nightcrawlers. These are the horrors that plague John's slumber. The senseless images in his psyche become apparent and the macabre mental puzzle is solved. John is awakened by an epiphany that strikes him like lightning. Sitting up in bed, he yells, "I know where she is! I can't believe I didn't see it before! I know where she is,

Emma!" John's words echo throughout the house like a victorious battle cry. Lights all over the house start illuminating the windows as if a sleeping giant is coming to life. John is motivated and filled with determination; the final chapter of the mystery awaits, and there won't be another moment wasted.

His Carolina work boots are laced up tight, and cowhide tan gloves are in his back denim pocket. He exits through the back door, unlocking the shed. John grabs a lantern, a spade shovel, and his wheelbarrow. All the tools are thrown into the bed of his pickup truck, and he cranks the engine. Within seconds, the truck has made its way to the barn, shining its headlights on the front swinging doors. "The horses," he thinks to himself.

It's 3:00 a.m. on Gentry Farm, and the witching hour is unsettled. John swings the barn doors open, grabs his shovel and wheelbarrow, and hurries into the barn that has held the darkest secret for all these years. Shovelfuls of dirt fill the wheelbarrow from the first stable until it's full. Then, he dumps the earth behind the barn. For hours, the sound of the spade striking the earth spills out of the barn. Nothing. The next stable starts being wildly excavated. John heaves shovelfuls of dirt over and over. Muscles strain from labor, and sweat pours from his brow.

Crows have gathered in the lifeless oak tree to witness the secret revealed. The crescent moon illuminates the silhouette of each crow sitting stoically and still on the branches.

The spade strikes the earth, but this time a different noise spills from the barn. The shovel hits something about four feet deep in the second stable. John gets down on his knees and begins to sift dirt away from something. The lantern lights up the stable, and John sees what lies beneath the dirt. A small child's fractured skull looks back at him as if to say, "You finally found me." At this moment, the murder of crows takes flight into the night with caws of jubilation and rejoicing.

Accompanying the skull is a complete skeleton that belonged to baby Meredith Gentry. Emotion overtakes John as he weeps uncontrollably. Climbing out of the grave, exhaustion overcomes his body. Covered in black earth and feeling like a weary gravedigger, he looks out into the open pasture. A beautiful apparition of Mabel is peering back at John. The smile and the eyes of a soul finally at rest thank John without words. Mabel holds the lost love she has mourned, even after death. Meredith has her arms around her mother's neck and now rests forever, eternally. A radiant and heavenly glow emanates from the two spirits, described only as God's light. Mabel slowly turns around, takes three steps, and fades into oblivion. From that moment on, mother and daughter spend eternity together in the grace and light of God's love.

John prays and weeps tears of pure joy and relief. Never in his life has he ever accomplished a task so significant and important. Never has John felt joy and peace as he did at that moment. He felt and saw the love and gratitude in Mabel's eyes. She would no longer be in torment.

Chapter Twelve

Emma is beside herself with emotion and relief when John returns from the barn, filthy and exhausted. They decide that prayer is a priority before anything else is done. Only after will phone calls be made and the authorities informed.

The farm becomes awash with sheriff vehicles and first responders as word spreads that baby Meredith has finally been found. Emergency lights from ambulances and law enforcement vehicles paint the property red and blue. Every Ohio law enforcement officer and crime scene technician arrives at Gentry Farm. No matter how hardened or grizzled the individual on the scene appeared to be, upon sight and confirmation of the unearthed remains of baby Meredith, everyone breaks down and sheds tears of joy and sorrow.

Investigators and analysts from all medical and criminal justice disciplines occupy the barn for hours. Camera flashes illuminate the inside of the barn like strobe lights for most of the day. The investigator taking the report is baffled to learn that John got the idea to dig in the barn from recurring nightmares he had since moving onto the farm.

Emma called Aunt Ruth early that morning to tell her about the discovery, but when Ruth answered the phone, her first words were, "He found her in the barn, didn't he?" Ruth was born with a gift that amazed everyone who had ever known her.

Two weeks passed, and after every test imaginable—from DNA testing to pathology reports and autopsies—a private funeral ceremony took place at Rose Hill Memorial Gardens. Only a handful of attendees paid their respects and prayed for closure and healing. John and Emma's neighbor, along with one of the original search and rescue volunteers from all those years ago, were in attendance. Bunk stood solemn and silent throughout the entire service. Everyone knew he had finally found the peace and closure he had needed all these years. Aunt Ruth attended the service and held hands with Emma the entire time. This support was essential to both Emma and John. Only a few of baby Meredith's family members attended, all from Mabel's side of the family. No one from Theo Gentry's side attended the service.

After all the pieces of the puzzle were put into place, the picture of what happened to baby Meredith became clear and heart breaking. The autopsy report showed that baby Meredith died from blunt force trauma to the head. The skull fracture was consistent with the toddler being thrown down the stairs. While it cannot be proven all these years later, it is known by a few that in a drunken and abusive rage against Mabel, Theodore Gentry threw his daughter down the stairs because she would not stop crying. Meredith died soon after receiving her injuries at the bottom of the staircase.

The energy of Gentry Farm has changed from a dark and gloomy feel to a peaceful and tranquil ambiance. Optimism and joy have taken up residence on Gentry Farm after several decades of hopelessness and sorrow infecting the property.

Emma gave birth to a healthy, seven-pound, twelve-ounce baby girl six and a half months later. The baby looks just like Emma did in her baby pictures, even having Emma's gorgeous green eyes. John decided on one name immediately, and Emma put up no fight. They named their newborn baby girl Meredith Grace.

Made in the USA
Middletown, DE
02 July 2024